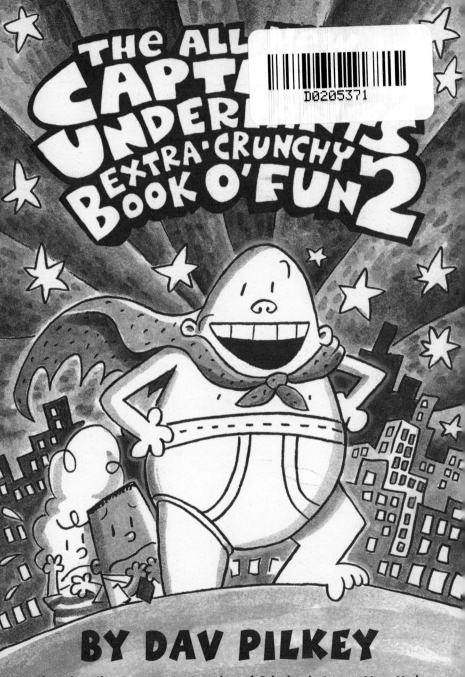

THE ALL NEW CAPTAIN UNDERPANTS EXTRA-CRUNCHY BOOK O' FUN 2

BY DAV PILKEY

The Blue Sky Press • An Imprint of Scholastic Inc. • New York

For Elizabeth and Rachel

THE BLUE SKY PRESS

No part of this publication may be reproduced in whole or in part, or
stored in a retrieval system, or transmitted in any form or by any means,
electronic, mechanical, photocopying, recording, or otherwise, without
written permission of the publisher. For information regarding permission,
please write to: Permissions Department, Scholastic Inc.,
557 Broadway, New York, New York 10012.

CAPTAIN UNDERPANTS is a registered trademark of Dav Pilkey.
SCHOLASTIC, THE BLUE SKY PRESS, and associated logos are
trademarks and/or registered trademarks of Scholastic Inc.

Be sure to check out Dav Pilkey's
Extra-Crunchy Web Site O' Fun at www.pilkey.com

ISBN 0-439-37608-4

12 11 10 9 8 7 6 5   2 3 4 5 6 7/0

Printed in the United States of America   40
First printing, September 2002

WEDGIE-POWERED WORD FIND

Try to find the names below in the puzzle on the right.
Look up, down, backwards, and diagonally.

CHARACTER NAME BONUS QUIZ:

How well do you know your UNDERPANTS?
Draw lines from the <u>first</u> names in Chart A
to the matching <u>last</u> names in Chart B.

CHART A	CHART B
Benny	Beard
Billy	Fyde
George	Hoskins
Harold	Hutchins
Melvin	Krupp
Morty	Poopypants
Pippy	Ribble
Tara	Sneedly
Tippy	Tinkletrousers

```
S T N A P Y P O O P
R U O R L Y H Q N A
E G N L V X T V F F
S N I H C T U H L Z
U B V M A L O E S A
O A L F O S G D R J
R U E C K R R A Q E
T F M I O A T D D I
E S N E E D L Y V E
L S G B L O F L R S
K Q F F R B P C P U
N S E A E R B I C R
I A H N Y P P I T Z
T X N M J P P U R K
K Y Q B Y R Z X D C
```

(Answer on page 93)

HOW TO DRAW
CAPTAIN UNDERPANTS

1.

2.

3.

4.

5.

6.

7.

8.

9.

10.

11.

12.

13.

14.

15.

16.

PERPLEXING PEEWEE-POWERED PUZZLE

ACROSS

3. Captain Underpants fights for Truth, Justice, and all that is Pre-Shrunk and _____!

5. A flushable porcelain bowl.

7. "Tra-_____-Laaaaa!"

8. Super Diaper Baby's archenemy is _____ Doo-Doo.

9. Captain Underpants is nicknamed the _____ Warrior.

10. Super Diaper Baby's best friend is Diaper _____.

11. The only five-letter word (starting with an "s") to appear twice in the last six clues.

14. Watch out for the Wicked Wedgie _____!

15. Liquid spray _____ is the enemy of underwear.

DOWN

1. The three evil space guys were named _____, Klax, and Jennifer.

2. New Swissland's most famous scientist is Professor _____.

3. Three cheers for _____ Underpants!

4. The Bride of _____ Potty.

6. Beware of the _____-Toilet 2000!

10. Billy Hoskins is better known as Super _____ Baby.

12. Don't spill the Extra-Strength Super _____ Juice!

13. Ms. _____ turned into the Wicked Wedgie Woman.

(Answer on page 93)

HOW TO DRAW
MR. KRUPP

1.

2.

3.

4.

5.

6.

7.

8.

9.

10.

11.

12.

13.

14.

15.

16.

Help George and Harold Get into Their Tree House

START HERE

END HERE

(Answer on page 94)

Q) Why did the cookie cry?
A) Because his mom had been a wafer so long.

"Knock knock."
"Who's there?"
"Olive Toop."
"Olive Toop who?"
"Well so do I, but you don't hear *me* braggin' about it!"

Ms. Ribble: Harold, if I gave you two goldfish, and Melvin gave you four goldfish, how many would you have?
Harold: Eleven.
Ms. Ribble: *ELEVEN*?!!? Hah! You're *WRONG*, bub!
Harold: No, *you're* wrong. I already have five goldfish back at home!

George: Excuse me, mister, I'd like to buy some toilet paper.
Grocery store clerk: What color would you like?
George: Just give me white. I'll color it myself!

Q) What do you get when you cross a porcupine with a great white shark?
A) As far away as possible.

HOW TO DRAW GEORGE

1.

2.

3.

4.

5.

6.

7.

8.

9.

10.

11.

12.

13.

14.

15.

16.

HOW TO DRAW HAROLD

1.

2.

3.

4.

5.

6.

7.

8.

9.

10.

11.

12.

13.

14.

15.

16.

NOW YOU CAN BE THE STAR
OF YOUR OWN SUPER-CHEESY
CAPTAIN UNDERPANTS STORY!

Before you read the story on the following pages, go through and find all the blanks. Below each blank is a small description of what you need to write in the blank. Just fill in the blank with an appropriate word.

For example, if the blank looks like this:

_____, you would think up an adjective and
(an adjective)

put it in the blank like this: ____*Snotty*____ .
(an adjective)

Remember, don't read the story first. It's more fun if you go through and fill in the blanks first, THEN read the story.

When you're done, follow the instructions at the bottom of each page to complete the illustrations. Cool, huh?

JUST FOR REMINDERS:
a **Verb** is an <u>action</u> word (like jump, swim, kick, squish, run, etc.)
an **Adjective** is a word that <u>describes</u> a person, place, or thing (lumpy, dumb, purple, hairy, etc.)

THE INCREDIBLY STUPID ADVENTURE OF
CAPTAIN UNDERPANTS

This is George Beard, Harold Hutchins,

and ___Jimmy___ ___Smale___.
       (your first name)   (your last name)

George is the one on the left with the tie and

the flat-top. Harold is the one on the right

with the T-shirt and the bad haircut.

___Jimmy___ is the one in the middle
(your first name)

with the ___shrik___ ___niced___
       (an adjective)   (article of clothing)

and the ___butt naked___ ___butt___.
       (an adjective)   (body part or parts)

Remember that now.

↑
(Draw yourself here)

One day, George, Harold, and _____
(your first name)

were at school when suddenly, an evil _____
(an adjective)

villain _____ through the door and
(a verb ending in "ed")

roared like a ferocious _____ .
(a harmless insect)

"My name is Commander_____
(a gross adjective)

_____ !" shouted the villain. "And I've come
(a gross thing)

to destroy all the _____ in the world!"
(smelly things)

Commander_____ _____
(the gross adjective and thing you used above)

grabbed a _____ and started hitting
(a piece of furniture)

_____ on the _____ with it.
(your gym teacher's name)   (a body part)

"Oh no!" cried_____ . "That villain is
(your first name)

going to hurt the poor _____ !"
(the piece of furniture you used above)

(Draw yourself here)   (Draw your evil villain here)

20

"We've got to stop that monster!" cried

George. He reached into his _____ ,
                                    (an article of clothing)

grabbed a/an _____ _____ ,
                   (an adjective)   (something big)

and threw it at the villain.

Harold found a/an _____ in his
                        (something bigger)

_____ , so he threw that, too. Finally,
(an article of clothing)

_____ reached into his/her _____ ,
(your name)   (an article of clothing)

pulled out a/an _____ _____ ,
                  (an adjective)   (the biggest thing you can think of)

and threw that as well.

But nothing seemed to stop the _____
                                (a disgusting adjective)

Commander _____ _____ !
           (the gross adjective and thing you used twice on page 20)

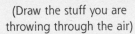

(Draw yourself here)   (Draw the stuff you are   (Draw your evil
                        throwing through the air)   villain here)

"This looks like a job for Captain Underpants!"

shouted _____.
(your first name)

Suddenly, Captain Underpants _____
(a verb ending in "ed")

into the school. "Hi," said Captain Underpants.

"How's your _____ _____
(an adjective)   (an animal)

_____ today?"
(a part of the body)

"That doesn't make any sense," said Harold.

"Who cares?" said _____. "We've got
(your first name)

to stop that villain!" So Captain Underpants

grabbed a baseball bat and hit Commander

_____ _____ over the
(the gross adjective and thing you used twice on page 20)

head repeatedly.

(Draw yourself here)   (Draw your evil villain here)

22

HERE COMES THE BAT, MAN!

(Draw your villain here. Make him about the same height
as Captain Underpants. If you need help, look at the
Flip-O-Ramas between pages 45 and 89 for inspiration.)

HERE COMES THE BAT, MAN!

(Draw your villain here. Make him about the same height
as Captain Underpants. If you need help, look at the
Flip-O-Ramas between pages 45 and 89 for inspiration.)

"Holy_____ _____!" shouted
(a verb ending in "ing")   (an animal)

George. "Captain Underpants has defeated

Commander_____ _____!"
(the gross adjective and thing you used twice on page 20)

"Let's celebrate by eating _____ servings of
(a number)

_____ _____ and drinking _____ cups
(an adjective)   (something gross)   (a number)

of _____ _____ ," said Harold.
(an adjective)   (a disgusting liquid)

"That sounds delicious," said _____ .
(your first name)

"Just be sure to sprinkle some_____
(a gross adjective)

_____ on my food, and add a slice of
(creepy things)

_____ to my_____."
(something gross)   (the disgusting liquid you used above)

(Draw yourself sitting here)   (Draw your defeated villain lying here)

26

(Answer on page 94)

HOW TO DRAW WEDGIE WOMAN

1.

2.

3.

4.

5.

6.

7.

8.

9.

10.

28

11.

12.

13.

14.

15.

16.

HOW TO DRAW ZORX, KLAX, AND JENNIFER

1.

2.

3.

4.

5.

6.

7.

8.

9.

10.

FUN WITH ACCESSORIES

1. Add eyelashes!

2. Add lipstick!

3. Add a bow!

Zorxette

4a.

4b.

Klaxette

5a.

5b.

Jenniferette

6a.

6b.

32

(Answer on page 95)

(Answer on page 95)

Q) Why does Ms. Ribble keep a stick of dynamite in her auto emergency kit?
A) In case she gets a flat and needs to blow up one of her tires.

Q) Why was the mushroom always invited to parties?
A) Because he was a fungi!

Q) What's the difference between Mr. Krupp and an elephant?
A) One is huge, wrinkled, has a goofy nose, and smells terrible . . . and the other is an elephant!

Q) What's green, cold, and topped with whipped cream?
A) A snot-fudge sundae.

Q) What's invisible and smells like bananas?
A) Monkey burps!

Q) What's the difference between pea soup and popcorn?
A) Anyone can pop corn!

Tommy: Mommy, can I lick the bowl?
Mommy: No, Tommy, you have to flush like everybody else!

the Night of the Terror of the Revenge of the Curse of the Bride of Hairy Potty

staring Captain underpants

with Super Diaper Baby

and Diaper Dog "(?)"

By George Beard and Harold Hutchins

PRO LOG

Our story began When a sientist created a Hair growth formula. ILL try it on a froggy 	But the formula made everything grow Big and hairy and evil! RiB-Bit HeLp! 
So he dumped the Formula down the toilet Bye Bye 	But he forgot to FLUSH .... WeLL thats is the end of that! 
The Toilet grew Big and hairy...	... and evil! Uh oh 

Hairy Potty exscaped and Reaked Havok.

Roar.

ZAP

But then captain Underpants came

Hey, Bub

and Saved the day

Bye Bye

uh-oh

CRASH

Hooray

Everybody thought it was the end ...but it was only the Begining!!!

Turn the page for Part **2**

The Night of the Terror of the Revenge of the Curse of the Bride of Hairy Potty

By George Beard and Harold Hutchins

Our story continyous at the scene of the crime. Worker guys were removing all the broken pieces of Hairy Potty.

Suddenly, this one guy showed up and stoled one of the ~~pos~~ pieces.

Hey stop

No way

He brought the Rib shaped piece back to his Labratory

Dr. Frank enbeanies secret Labratory

Haw Haw Haw

Jeff took his DNA extrackshon Lazer Phazer with him.

Soon he met a women

Excuse me, could you tell me where I can find a Lady?

?

I'm a Lady!

No, I mean a "Pretty" Lady.

You know... Someone who is Young and thin and...

WARNING

The Following Seene contains Extremly ~~grt~~ graphic Violins.

View at your own Risk →

FLiP·O·RAMA

HER'ES HOW it WORKS !!!!

STEP 1

Plase your Left Hand inside the doted Lines marked "LEFT HAND HERE" Hold the BOOK open FLAT

STEP 2

GRasp the Right-hand page with your Right Thumb and index Finger (inside the doted Lines MARKED "Right Thumb Here").

STEP 3

Now Quickly FLip The Right-hand page back and Fourth until the pitcher apears to be animated.

(For extra Fun, try adding your own Sound-Affecks!)

FLIP-O-RAMA #1

Pages 45 and 47.

Remember, Flip only page 45. While you are Fliping, be shure you can see the Pitcher on page 45 and the one on Page 47.

If you Flip Quickly, the two pitchers will start to Look like one Animated pitcher.

Left Hand Here

Smack Attack

RIGHT
THuMB
Here

Smack Attack

But the Lazer beam got REFLECKTED by her mirrer from her make-up Thingy.

The beam Shot UP in the air and got refleckted again off of a sign.

...and down it came...

The Beam extrackt-ed the DNA From a strand of hair.

YANK

Then it gave the hair to Jeff.

Hooray!

With The DNA in this single strand of your hair, We can create a monster!!!

huh?

Now ALL my Problems are over!

FLIP-O-RAMA

LeFT HAnd Here

I am woman,
see me punch

Right
thumb
Here

I am woman,
see me punch

Soon, Jeff Reterned to the Secret Lab

Did you get the DNA?

Yeah.

So DR. Frankenbeanies Put the hair into his cloning machine.

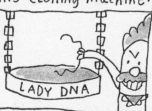

LADY DNA

where will we get the power to Run the machine?

LADY DNA

HAIRY POTTY DNA

From Lightning! ALL we have to do is Wait For a big Storm!

meanwhile, The city guys Finished cLeaning up the pieces from where Hairy Potty got killed.

Were aLL done.

Lets Dump this stuff and go home

Trash

O.K.

They drove the pieces to A Toxic ~~waste~~ waste dump.

Hurry up... A Storm is coming

Soon, a terible storm arosed. The Lightning struck Hairy Potty's pieces. It also struck the secret LAbratory. Sudenly, wierd things began to happen.

Hairy Potty's Pieces began to morph together.

And DR. Frankenbeanies cloning machine began to work.

With every flash, Hairy Potty morphed more and more.

... and Dr. Frankenbeanies experiment grew and grew.

strechy
strechy

RIGHT
ThumB
Here

Strechy
strechy

Left Hand Here

jumping rope
with a dope.

RiGHt
thum#B
Here

Jumping rope
with a dope.

Soon, she got tired of playing...

So she zapped a hole in the wall and exscaped.

I'm free!

THEATER
NOW SHOWING
BRiGET Jonses DiARY

Tee-Hee

NOW SHOWING
BRiGET Jonses DiARRHEA

meanwhile, on the very next Page, Hairy Potty was causing mischiff of his own...→

Finaly, the two Toilets met. It was Love at First site!!!

Hairy Potty took his new girlfrend out for a Lovley dinner of toilet Paper and Urinel cakes.

That very moment, Just a few blocks away...

we interupt This Program to bring you a speshel news thingy.

captain Underpants is getting his butt Kicked over on main STREET

who will save him??

we will

well hurry up, then!

And so Super Diaper BAby Flew to the Rescue...

SWOOOOSH

...with his best Friend Diaper Dog by his side.

soon they arived at the seeen.

So Super Diaper Baby Flew Captain Underpants up to a safe plase on top of a bilding. But Diaper Dog Flew home. He had a plan...

First he found a volleyball and a marker.	Then he drew his face on the volley ball.

Squeak

Squeak Squeak

squeak squeak

Then he flew back to the crime sceen with the ball and a bicicle tire pump.

ZOOM

Diaper Dog atached the bike pump to the ball and hid behind the bushes.

Come over here you weenie!

Hairy Potty WAS s-o mAd he grabbed the ball and ate it up.

then Diaper Dog started pumping.

What the?

FLiP -O- RAMA

LeFt Hand HeRe

Inflate-a-Bowl

RIGHt
ThumB
Here

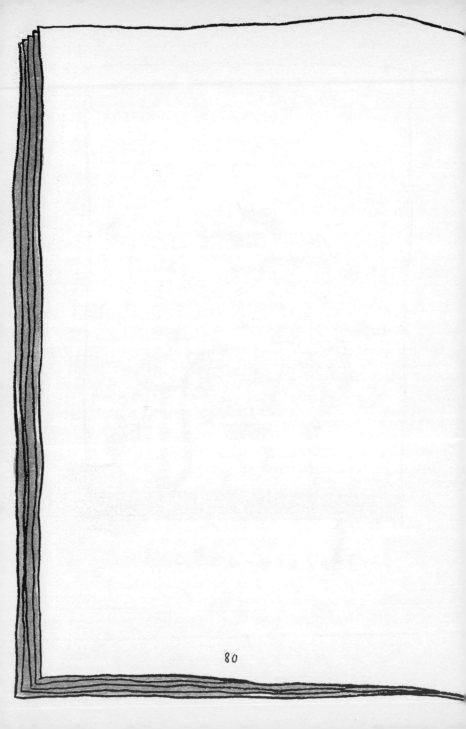

Inflate-a-Bowl

Sudenly, Super Diaper Baby FLEW into action from his secret hiding plase.

OH NO!!! Super Diaper Baby and Diaper Dog Both got eaten --- and Captain Underpants was still Too Weak to Fight. Is this the end for our heros?

Left Hand
Here

Hammer time

Right
thumB
Here

Hammer time

ANSWERS

Word Find
p. 4

```
S T N A P Y P O O P
R U O R L Y H Q N A
E G N L V X T V F F
S N I H C T U H L Z
U B V M A L O E S A
O A L F O S G D R J
R U E C K R R A Q E
T F M I O A T D D I
E S N E E D L Y V E
L S G B L O F L R S
K Q F F R B P C P U
N S E A E R B I C R
I A H N Y P P I T Z
T X N M J P P U R K
K Y Q B Y R Z X D C
```

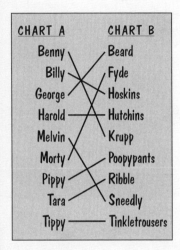

CHART A	CHART B
Benny	Beard
Billy	Fyde
George	Hoskins
Harold	Hutchins
Melvin	Krupp
Morty	Poopypants
Pippy	Ribble
Tara	Sneedly
Tippy	Tinkletrousers

Bonus Quiz
p. 4

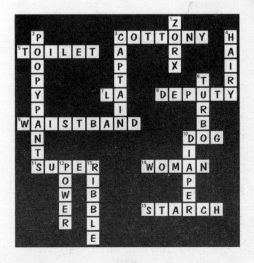

Crossword
p. 8

Maze p. 12

Maze p. 27

**Maze
p. 33**

**Maze
p. 34**